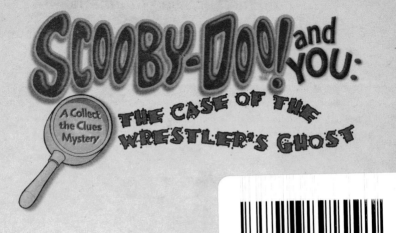

SCOOBY-DOO! and YOU:
THE CASE OF THE WRESTLER'S GHOST

A Collect the Clues Mystery

D0068649

By Tracey West

WORLDWIDE PUBLISHING™

SCHOLASTIC INC.
New York   Toronto   London   Auckland   Sydney
Mexico City   New Delhi   Hong Kong

*To my mother, who taught me
to love mysteries — and Scooby-Doo.*

ISBN 0-439-23152-3

12 11 10 9 8 7 6   2 3 4 5 6/0

Cover and interior illustrations by Duendes del Sur
Cover and interior design by Madalina Stefan

Printed in the U.S.A.

First Scholastic printing, December 2000

You've been waiting for a long time to check out this wrestling restaurant, named after famous wrestler Mondo Mitchell. Television screens showing wrestling matches line the walls. The waiters all wear wrestling costumes. Each table is surrounded by a wrestling ring.

But there's something in the restaurant you weren't expecting to see. The Scooby Gang! They're eating lunch at a nearby table. Daphne spots you and waves.

1

"Nice to see you again," she says. "Why don't you join us?"

You climb through the ring's ropes around their table and sit down. The gang is looking at their menus. A waiter wearing pink polka-dot tights approaches.

"Like, just give us one of everything on the menu," Shaggy tells him.

"*Re roo,*" Scooby-Doo says.

"Correction," Shaggy says. "*Two* of everything."

The waiter rolls his eyes and walks away.

"Malcom Mitchell, the restaurant owner, is treating us to a free meal," Velma explains. "We helped him solve a mystery."

Shaggy shudders. "Like, we even got chased by a ghost."

"Speaking of mysteries, I bet you'd like to read about the one we just solved," Fred says. He hands you a notebook. "I wrote all about it in the Clue Keeper."

You take the Clue Keeper from Fred.

"I wrote down all the details of the mystery in there," he tells you. "All the suspects and clues."

"You can try to figure out the mystery as you read," says Daphne.

"And don't forget, there are symbols in the Clue Keeper to help you," Velma says. " 👁 👁 means we found a suspect. And a 🔦 means we found a clue."

Fred hands you a pencil. "You'll need this, too. At the end of each entry, we wrote some questions to help you organize the clues and suspects you find."

You open the Clue Keeper to the first entry. Can you solve *The Case of the Wrestler's Ghost?*

Daphne smiles. "Don't worry. You're going to do great."

Clue Keeper Entry 1

"This is so exciting, Scoob!" Shaggy said. "I can't believe we're going to see Babyface Foster wrestle live and in person!"

"Rooray!" Scooby-Doo cheered. He flexed his arm muscles like a wrestler.

I pulled the Mystery Machine into the parking lot of the Headlock Hotel.

"Don't get too excited yet, guys," I told them. "The wrestling match isn't until tomorrow. We have to check into our hotel, first."

We took our luggage out of the van and headed for the hotel lobby. Velma had her head buried in a book about wrestling.

We walked up to the hotel desk. But before we could check in, a man ran into the lobby. He was hysterical.

"Somebody help!" the man cried. "It's terrible. Babyface Foster has been kidnapped!"

Kidnapped? This sounded like a mystery to me.

"Calm down," I told the man. "My name is Fred. Can you tell us what happened?"

The man took a deep breath. "I'm Malcolm Mitchell, owner of the Mondo Wrestling Association," he explained. "I was just in Babyface's room. It was a mess. I found this."

Malcolm Mitchell handed me a note. It read, *I have Babyface. Don't bother looking for him. He will be returned to you after tomorrow's main event.*

"Oh no!" Shaggy cried. "There won't *be* an event without Babyface."

Malcolm buried his face in his hands. "Don't I know it. Without a main event, tomorrow, I'll be ruined."

"You must be worried that Babyface is in danger," Daphne said.

"Of course," said Malcolm. "Babyface hasn't been too happy lately. And now this happens!"

"Don't worry, Mr. Mitchell," I said. "My friends and I can help." I told him about how we had solved mysteries before.

"It would be great if you could find Babyface!" Malcolm Mitchell said. "I'm desperate. I've got to find him by tomorrow."

"If it isn't just like my big brother, messing things up again," a voice said.

I turned around. The voice belonged to a dark-haired woman. She looked like Malcolm, but her features were a bit sharper. And her suit was crisp and clean.

"This isn't my fault, Maxine," Malcolm said.

"It's never your fault, is it?" she replied. She held out a hand to shake. "Maxine Mitchell," she introduced herself. "My dear, departed father left Malcolm in charge of the Mondo Wrestling Association. Malcolm's done nothing but mess things up ever since Daddy died."

Malcolm's face turned beet-red.

"Do you work for the MWA, too?" Velma asked.

"I'm the head of publicity," Maxine replied. "And even though it's not a big job, it's better than the job Malcolm wanted me to have — head of makeup. Luckily I'm allergic to the stuff. Can you imagine? Me, head of makeup! I should be running the whole association."

"We don't want any publicity about this kidnapping," Malcolm told his sister. "I want that arena packed tomorrow. People have to think Babyface will be there."

Maxine smiled a thin smile. "Whatever you say, brother," she said. "If you blow this one, then maybe everyone will see who *really* deserves to be in charge." She walked away.

Beads of sweat formed on Malcolm's forehead. "I'm counting on you kids," he said. "You've got to do this for me."

"Like, we won't let you down," Shaggy said. "Babyface is my favorite wrestler."

I looked at Shaggy, Scooby, Daphne, and Velma. "Well, gang," I said, "it looks like we have a mystery to solve!"

"Did you catch the 👀 on page 7? We thought you would. That means we've found our first suspect. Answer these questions about this suspect in your Clue Keeper notebook."

1. What is the suspect's name?

2. What does she do for a living?

3. Why might she have kidnapped Babyface Foster?

Clue Keeper Entry 2

We quickly checked into our rooms. Then Malcolm Mitchell took us to the scene of the crime. "Good luck," he said as he left.

The room was a mess, just like Malcolm had said. Velma combed the area with her magnifying glass.

"No luck," Velma said finally. "But I did notice a video monitor in the hallway. Maybe that will show us something."

"Good idea," I said. Malcolm returned and took us to the hotel security office. The security officer was happy to help.

"I found the note about three o'clock this

afternoon," Malcolm told him. "And I spoke to Babyface in his room fifteen minutes earlier. So the kidnapping had to have happened during those fifteen minutes."

"Right," the security officer said. "I'll start it at two forty-five." She hit some buttons on a control pad. A black-and-white picture appeared on a monitor. It showed an empty hallway. The door to Babyface's room was clearly visible. Nothing happened for a few minutes.

Then, slowly, the door opened.

A big, muscular man stepped out.

He had a black handlebar mustache. He wore a leopard-patterned wrestling outfit.

But there was something strange about him. Very strange.

His skin glowed with an eerie light — at least the part of his skin that showed beneath the mask he wore that covered the top half of his face.

Malcolm Mitchell went pale. "Oh, my gosh," he said, falling into a chair. "That's my great-grandfather, Mondo Mitchell. He's a g-g—"

"A ghost!" Shaggy cried. Scooby-Doo jumped into Shaggy's arms. "Like, we're out of here."

"Calm down, guys," I said. "Are you sure that's him?"

Malcolm nodded. "I know exactly what he looked like. Everyone around here does. Mondo's picture is all over everything in the MWA. The federation is named after him."

"Are you saying that a ghost kidnapped Babyface?" Daphne asked.

"It looks that way," Velma said.

At that moment, there was a loud knock on the door.

The door swung open. A tall man stepped inside the office. He had wavy black hair and a beard. He wore a black T-shirt and black jeans.

Shaggy and Scooby hid behind Daphne. "This guy's scarier than a ghost," Shaggy whispered. "It's Simon Blackheart!"

Simon nodded. "That's right. I heard some kids were helping to find Babyface Foster. Is there any sign of him?"

Simon was an interesting character, I thought. He looked scary. But he had a friendly voice and seemed really nice.

"Nothing yet," I told him. "But we're working on it."

Simon's face clouded. "Gee, I hope nothing bad happens to him."

Shaggy looked shocked. "But, like, I thought you guys hated each other. You're supposed to wrestle each other in the big event tomorrow."

Simon smiled. "That's just in the ring. Outside the ring, we're pretty good friends. I was real upset when I heard he'd been kidnapped."

"We'll let you know if we find out anything, Mr. Blackheart," I told him.

"Thanks," Simon said. "I'll be in the makeup room at the arena if you need me.

I'm shooting a commercial in a little while."
He left the office.

"He seemed so nice," Daphne said.

"I wouldn't be too sure," Velma warned. She turned to Malcolm Mitchell. "Weren't Babyface and Simon supposed to wrestle for the championship tomorrow?"

Malcolm nodded.

"And what happens if Babyface doesn't show up for the match?" Velma asked.

"Well, Babyface would forfeit. Simon would win the championship automatically," he said.

"Very interesting," said Velma. She turned to me. "I think I'd like to have another talk with this Simon Blackheart!"

"Hey, did you see the back on page 14? You've found another suspect! Answer these questions in your Clue Keeper notebook:"

 1. What is the potential suspect's name?

 2. What does he do for a living?

 3. Why might he have kidnapped Babyface Foster?

Clue Keeper Entry 3

"Let's split up, gang," I suggested. "Velma and Daphne, you talk to Simon Blackheart. Shaggy and Scooby and I will see if we can find anything more here in the hotel."

I looked at my watch. "Let's meet in an hour for dinner."

"An hour!" Shaggy cried. Scooby's stomach rumbled.

Velma and Daphne headed out to the arena next door.

Scooby, Shaggy, and I took the elevator to the top floor. I looked up and down the hallway.

"I'll start at that end," I said. "And you two can start — Shaggy? Scooby?"

Shaggy and Scooby were walking down the hallway. In front of them, a bellhop held a silver room service tray. Shaggy and Scooby sniffed the air. Whatever was under that tray had a strong smell. It was irresistible to Shaggy and Scooby.

The bellhop stopped in front of room 1310. Shaggy grabbed the tray from him.

"Mmmm, liver and onions," Shaggy said. "Just like Aunt Hilda used to make."

Suddenly, the door to room 1310 swung open. A small man with thinning hair and glasses glared at Shaggy and Scooby.

"It's about time," he said, taking the tray. He started to close the door.

"Hey!" Shaggy stopped him. "Aren't you Tim Bender? Owner of the National Wrestling Group?"

"That's right," the man said. "Now if you'll excuse me —" He started to close the door again.

I stopped him. "Excuse me, sir, I was just

wondering. Isn't your wrestling organization in competition with the MWA?"

Tim Bender frowned. "So?" Then he slammed the door in my face.

"What a coincidence!" Shaggy said. "I bet Tim Bender would be happy if he knew Babyface Foster was kidnapped. If there's no big event tomorrow, the MWA could be ruined. He'd, like, have no more competition."

"I wonder if it *is* a coincidence?" I said.

"Like, did you see the on page 19? Groovy. Write down the answers to these questions in your Clue Keeper note-book while Scooby and I go look for a snack."

1. What is the potential suspect's name?

2. What does he do for a living?

3. Why might he have kidnapped Babyface Foster?

21

Clue Keeper Entry 4

We searched the hotel from top to bottom. Everything seemed normal. We didn't find any sign of Babyface Foster — or the ghost of Mondo Mitchell.

Finally, we were back in the hotel lobby.

"Like, where are the girls?" Shaggy asked. "I'm getting weak from hunger."

"*Re roo,*" Scooby-Doo agreed.

"It's not like the girls to be late," I admitted. "Maybe we should walk over to the arena and make sure they're all right."

"Good idea," Shaggy said. "And I have an even better idea. Scooby and I will go to the hotel restaurant and start on dinner."

Scooby nodded his head eagerly.

"Oh, all right," I said.

I stepped outside the hotel. There was a special walking trail from the hotel to the arena. Overhead, stars twinkled in the early night sky.

Later on, Shaggy told me what happened after I left him and Scooby.

They started to go to the restaurant. But then they felt guilty about not coming with me. "What if the ghost of Mondo Mitchell is out there somewhere?" Shaggy had wondered. "They might need our help."

Scooby agreed that following me was the right thing to do. They ran out of the hotel and into the dark night.

In the distance, they saw a flash of white. Shaggy thought it was the white shirt I always wear. "Hey, Freddie!" Shaggy called out. "Like, wait for us!"

The white figure stopped. Then it moved closer. And closer.

"We changed our minds, Fred," Shaggy

said. "We couldn't leave you out here with
a — ghost!" Shaggy's voice turned into a
scream.

"Rhost!" Scooby yelled.

I heard their screams and I turned
around. I couldn't believe what I saw.

It was the ghost of Mondo Mitchell! A tall,
muscled man with glowing white skin was
chasing Shaggy and Scooby. He wore leopard-
skin and had a handlebar mustache.

The ghost chased Shaggy and Scooby up the trail, right toward me. I thought fast.

I jumped off the trail and hid behind a bush. When Shaggy and Scooby ran by, I pulled them off the trail.

The ghost stopped and looked around. Then he spoke in an eerie, deep voice.

"Let this be a warning," the ghost said. "Stop looking for Babyface Foster. Leave the Headlock Hotel tonight!"

Clue Keeper Entry 5

We slowly came out from behind the bush. The ghost was gone.

Shaggy and Scooby began walking back to the hotel.

"Where are you going?" I asked them.

"Like, if the ghost dude wants us to go, then we'll go," Shaggy said. "We can eat on the road."

"Rat's right!" Scooby added.

"What about Babyface Foster?" I asked. "I thought he was your hero."

Shaggy said. "I guess you're right, Freddie. We can't let down Babyface. But let's, like, stick together from now on, okay?"

"Sure," I said. "Let's go find the girls."

We walked down the trail to the stadium, a tall, white, circular building. Bright lights lit Mondo Mitchell Arena against the dark sky.

Daphne and Velma stepped out of the arena entrance.

"Sorry we're late," Daphne said.

"That's all right," I said. I told her about our meeting with the ghost of Mondo Mitchell.

"How did your talk go with Simon Blackheart?" I asked them.

"Simon Blackheart might be a villain in the ring, but he's a sweetheart in real life," Daphne said. "He seems very concerned about Babyface."

"In fact, he made an interesting comment," Velma said. "He said Babyface hadn't seemed very happy lately."

"Malcolm Mitchell said the same thing," I recalled.

Velma turned on her flashlight. "I'd love to look around and see if we can find out something about that ghost," she said.

Shaggy groaned. "Aren't we ever going to eat dinner?"

"It won't take long," Daphne said. "It's on the way back to the hotel, anyway."

"Okay," Shaggy sighed.

Velma led the way with her flashlight. "Where exactly did you see the ghost?"

Shaggy shuddered. "Like, Scooby and I had just stepped out on the trail."

Scooby raised his arms in the air, like a ghost. He pretended to chase Shaggy.

"Then I saw them," I jumped in. "I pulled them off the trail behind that bush."

Velma examined the bush closely. Everything was quiet, except for the rumbling of Shaggy's stomach.

Then Velma spoke. "Aha! Look at this!"

We gathered around the bush. Some of the leaves were smeared with a shiny, white substance.

Velma touched the leaves. "It's stage makeup. The kind actors use."

"Or wrestlers," Daphne added.

"This case just got a lot more interesting," I said. I turned to Shaggy and Scooby. "I guess we can finally go have dinner."

Shaggy and Scooby were way ahead of me. They were running toward the hotel.

"Last one to the restaurant is a wrestler's ghost!" Shaggy called behind him.

Velma's Mystery-Solving Tips

"**D**id you see the on page 28? That's your first clue. Write down the clue in your Clue Keeper. Then answer these questions:"

1. What clue did you find in this entry?

2. What does this clue tell you about the kidnapping?

3. Which suspect might have left this clue?

Clue Keeper Entry 6

We talked about the case during dinner. I told Daphne and Velma all about Tim Bender — owner of the rival wrestling organization — who was staying in the hotel.

Shaggy and Scooby didn't do much talking. They had their mouths full of french fries, bacon cheeseburgers, salad, clam chowder, and three whole pies.

We were all pretty tired after our long day. Shaggy, Scooby and I sacked out in our room. Velma and Daphne had the room next door.

I fell asleep as soon as my head hit the pillow. But I wasn't asleep for long.

"Zoinks!" a familiar voice cried. "Like, heeeeeeeeelp!"

I sat up and opened my eyes. Shaggy and Scooby's beds were empty.

I ran into the hall. Shaggy and Scooby were speeding down the hallway.

Shaggy slowed down and looked back at me. "Freddie! It's the ghost of Mondo Mitchell!" he said, breathing heavily.

I peered down the hallway. A flash of white disappeared around the corner.

"Stay here," I told them. I ran after the figure.

When I turned the corner, I ended up right in front of the elevators. The doors were closing in front of me.

I pressed the buttons, but it was no use. The ghost — if that was the ghost — was gone.

Shaggy and Scooby ran up behind me. Velma and Daphne came with them, looking sleepy.

"What exactly happened?" I asked Shaggy.

"Like, Scooby-Doo and I were in the mood for a midnight snack," Shaggy explained.

"After that huge dinner you had?" Daphne asked.

"That was hours ago," Shaggy said. He

patted his stomach. "Then my stomach started rumbling. Scooby and I thought we'd sneak out to the kitchen so we wouldn't disturb Freddie here."

"*Right!*" said Scooby.

"We were on our way when Mondo's ghost jumped out and started chasing us," Shaggy said. I looked at the lit-up panel above the elevator. The elevator had stopped on the thirteenth floor.

"Maybe it's not gone yet," I said. "I'm going up to the thirteenth floor and checking it out."

"I'll go with you," Velma offered.

"I'm not leaving the room again," Shaggy said. "Not until the sun comes up. Right, Scoob?"

Scooby nodded.

"I'll wait here with you until Fred and Velma come back," Daphne offered.

The elevator opened up in front of us. Velma and I went up to the thirteenth floor.

"It sure is quiet up here," Velma said.

"Maybe not so quiet," I said. A door was closing down the hall. Room 1310.

Tim Bender's room.

I ran to the door and stopped it from closing.

Tim Bender was wearing a robe. He glared at me through his glasses.

"Excuse me, Mr. Bender," I said. "There have been some suspicious things happening around here tonight. Did you see anyone come off the elevator just now?"

Tim Bender opened the door a little wider to reveal that he was holding a silver room service tray.

"It was probably just the bellboy," he said.

I recognized the smell coming from the tray. "More liver and onions?" I asked.

Tim Bender scowled. "It's very late, young man. Now if you'll excuse me." He slammed the door in my face.

Velma raised her eyebrows. "He's not in a very good mood, is he?" she asked.

"It must be from eating all that liver and onions," I said. "That would put me in a bad mood."

Velma and I went back to our rooms and we finally settled in for the night.

At breakfast the next morning, we decided what to do.

"The big wrestling event's just a few hours away," Shaggy said, between mouthfuls of waffles. "And we're not even close to finding Babyface."

"I think we've got some good leads," Velma said. "I'd like to talk to Simon Blackheart again. He has the easiest access to the makeup room. Maybe he's disguising himself as the ghost."

"That ghost looked pretty real to me," Shaggy said.

Scooby nodded. *"Real!"*

"I think talking to Simon again is a good idea," I said. "Let's head over to the arena. He'll probably be there getting ready for the event."

"If we don't find Babyface, there won't be an event," Shaggy said glumly.

We headed over to the arena. Velma and Daphne led us to the makeup room in the arena basement. As we got closer, we saw there was a big commotion in front of a room marked WARDROBE ROOM.

A blond wrestler wearing a bathrobe was yelling at Simon Blackheart and a group of wrestlers.

"I'm not leaving until somebody gives me my costume!" the wrestler screamed.

I walked up to the wrestlers.

"Is there some sort of problem?" I asked.

"My leopard-skin outfit is gone," said the wrestler. "I can't wrestle without it!"

"Can't you wrestle in something else?" Daphne suggested.

The wrestler's face turned beet-red. "Don't you know who I am?" he screamed. "I am Jungle Boy! Jungle Boy always wears leopard skin."

"Calm down, JB," Simon Blackheart told him. "Why are you so sure one of us stole it?"

"I had the costume cleaned yesterday morning. Then I locked it in the wardrobe room. You guys all have keys," Jungle Boy said accusingly.

"Yeah, but we all have our own costumes," Simon said. "We don't need yours."

That quieted Jungle Boy a little bit. "I

guess," he said. "But if nobody stole my costume, then where is it?"

"That's a very good question," Velma
whispered to me. "If we knew the answer,
we'd also know who kidnapped Babyface
Foster!"

"Did you see the 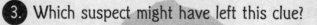 on page 37? We found another clue. Man, that Jungle Boy character is pretty steamed. While we're waiting for him to cool down, you can answer these questions in your Clue Keeper."

1. What clue did you find in this entry?

2. What does this clue have to do with the kidnapping?

3. Which suspect might have left this clue?

Clue Keeper Entry 7

Velma checked the wardrobe room for signs of a break-in.

"It looks pretty clean to me," Velma said. "Whoever took the costume must have had a key — or knew how to get one."

Simon Blackheart managed to calm down Jungle Boy. But another commotion sprang up.

Malcolm Mitchell stormed down the hallway. His sister Maxine walked behind him, smiling coolly.

"This is a disaster! A disaster!" Malcolm

said. He turned to us. "Have you kids found Babyface Foster yet?"

"Not yet," Velma said. "But we're getting close. We've found some good clues."

Malcolm sank into a folding chair and buried his face in his hands. "Things couldn't be worse," he said. He shot a look at his sister. "Somehow, the press has found out that Babyface was kidnapped."

Maxine smiled innocently. "I don't know how that could have happened, brother. Besides, what are you worried about? The stands are already filled with fans."

Malcolm groaned. "Great. That crowd will tear me to pieces if Babyface doesn't wrestle Simon in the main event. I'll have to give all that money back."

"How long 'til the main event?" I asked.

"About two hours," Maxine said. "There are always a few other matches before the big event. They get the crowd warmed up."

Two hours. We had solved mysteries in less time than that. I turned to the gang.

"Let's stick with our plan," I said. "Velma and Daphne, you find Simon and question him one more time. Shaggy and Scooby, why don't you come back to the hotel with me? I want to talk to Tim Bender again."

"Tim Bender!" Malcolm said, shocked. "What's he doing here?"

"That's what I'd like to find out," I said.

Shaggy, Scooby, and I walked outside the arena. Wrestling fans were pouring into the stadium. Reporters and camera crews were staked out outside.

A man carrying a microphone prepared for his newscast. We paused to listen.

"This is Les Powers, reporting from the Mondo Mitchell arena," he said. "We've just found out that Babyface Foster, who's scheduled to wrestle in today's main event, was kidnapped from the Headlock Hotel yesterday afternoon."

A crowd started to gather around the reporter. People listened intently.

"Babyface Foster, the current champion of the MWA, has been a fan favorite for many years," he continued. "He is best known for giving advice to his young fans. He always tells kids to look both ways before crossing the street, and to eat their liver and onions so they can grow big and strong."

Liver and onions? "Shaggy, did you know about this?" I asked.

"Sure, Freddie," Shaggy replied. "Babyface eats liver and onions for breakfast, lunch, and dinner. It's, like, his trademark."

The reporter finished his story. "Will Babyface Foster be found before today's big event? That's what these fans want to know."

Things were coming together. I ran back to the arena entrance.

"Hey, Freddie, wait for us!" Shaggy called. He and Scooby-Doo raced behind me.

I found Velma and Daphne talking to Malcolm Mitchell. I told them what the reporter had said about Babyface Foster liking liver and onions.

Velma got a gleam in her eye. "If you're thinking what I'm thinking, then I think we've got our mystery solved."

I nodded and turned to Malcolm Mitchell.

"Don't worry," I said. "We'll find Babyface's kidnapper before the big event. We all need to work together."

I gathered the gang around me. "Okay," I began, "here's our plan. . . ."

"We found an important clue in this chapter. Make sure you answer all of the questions about it."

 1. What clue did you find in this entry?

2. What do you think the clue has to do with the kidnapping?

3. Which suspect does this clue point to?

Clue Keeper Entry 8

Malcolm Mitchell agreed to our plan. We needed to get the ghost of Mondo to make an appearance at the big event.

"Let me get this straight," Shaggy said. "You actually *want* that spooky ghost to appear? Like, count me out!"

"Re roo!" Scooby agreed.

"Would you do it for a Scooby Snack?" Daphne asked him. She took a Snack from her purse.

Scooby shook his head again.

"Would you do it for two Scooby Snacks?" Velma asked.

Daphne held out another Snack.

Scooby hesitated. Then he slurped up the Scooby Snacks in one bite.

"Rokay!" Scooby said.

Shaggy turned to me. "Let's get this over with."

Daphne, Velma, and I waited backstage as Malcolm Mitchell led Shaggy and Scooby out into the arena.

Fireworks exploded as Malcolm walked to the wrestling ring. The crowd burst into applause.

Malcolm, Shaggy, and Scooby climbed into the ring. A ring announcer handed Malcolm a microphone.

"Good afternoon, ladies and gentlemen," Malcolm said, "and welcome to the Mondo Mitchell Arena!"

The crowd cheered and clapped. When they quieted down, Malcolm continued.

"I know many of you have heard the rumor that Babyface Foster has been kidnapped," Malcolm said. The crowd booed. "I want to tell you all not to worry."

Malcolm pointed to Shaggy and Scooby. "These fine detectives here have solved the case. Before the main event, they will reveal the name of Babyface's kidnapper."

Shaggy and Scooby waved to the crowd.

"And now," Malcolm said, "let's get ready to wrestle!"

Malcolm led Shaggy and Scooby out of the ring and backstage.

"You looked great out there," Daphne told Shaggy and Scooby.

"Now all we have to do is wait," I said. "You two sit here, by the entrance to the arena. Daphne and Velma will be in the makeup room. I'll be in the wardrobe room. If you see Mondo's ghost, just yell."

"Like, no problem!" Shaggy said.

From my position in the wardrobe room, I could see Shaggy and Scooby in their seats. There was also a television monitor, so I could watch what was going on in the ring.

If our plan worked, Babyface's kidnapper would try to stop Shaggy and Scooby from revealing what they knew. When the ghost appeared to nab Shaggy and Scooby, we would rush out and nab the ghost.

I watched the wrestling matches as we waited for the ghost to appear. I began to get nervous. It was almost time for the big event. What if the plan didn't work?

I looked at the TV screen. Jungle Boy was climbing into the ring. He was wearing purple-flowered tights, and he didn't look too happy about it. His opponent, the Bumblebee, climbed into the ring after him.

And then it happened.

I heard a door slam behind me. I pulled on the handle. Locked tight.

Outside, I heard screams.

"Like, gang, where are you?" Shaggy yelled.

"*Relp!*" Scooby cried.

I spun around and looked at the monitor.

Shaggy and Scooby were running down the aisle, toward the wrestling ring. A glowing figure chased them.

The ghost of Mondo Mitchell!

Shaggy and Scooby had nowhere to run. They climbed into the wrestling ring. Jungle Boy and the Bumblebee stopped in their tracks.

Mondo's ghost climbed into the ring next. He picked up Jungle Boy and twirled him around in the air. Then he threw Jungle Boy to one corner of the ring.

The Bumblebee climbed onto the top rope

of the ring. "Beware the Bumblebee's sting!" he yelled.

The Bumblebee jumped off the rope, and aimed right for Mondo's ghost.

The ghost caught Bumblebee in mid-flight. He held him in a headlock, then tossed Bumblebee out of the ring.

Shaggy and Scooby huddled together in the corner of the ring.

Mondo's ghost turned and faced Jungle Boy. A low growl came from his throat. He threw Jungle Boy into the audience.

"Ruh-roh," said Scooby.

"Like, what do we do now, Scooby?" Shaggy asked.

"*Restle*?" Scooby-Doo suggested.

Mondo's ghost stomped across the ring.

"I guess we don't have any choice!" Shaggy said.

Shaggy jumped up. Scooby climbed on to Shaggy's back. Shaggy ran in circles around the ring. Mondo's ghost chased him. "I call this move the 'chicken run,'" Shaggy said.

Mondo's ghost started to get dizzy. He stopped in the center of the ring, and he reeled back and forth.

"Okay, Scooby," Shaggy said. "Time to finish him off!"

"Right!" Scooby pounced on Mondo's ghost. The big ghost fell backward onto the mat. Scooby licked his face with his doggy tongue.

Mondo's ghost pounded the mat with his fists.

"Stop! That tickles!" said the ghost. His voice sounded different now.

"Like, do you give up?" Shaggy asked.

"Yes! Yes!" said the ghost. "I can't take it anymore."

Just then, I heard the door to the wardrobe room open. It was Simon Blackheart, holding a door key. Daphne, Velma, and Malcolm Mitchell stood behind him.

"Let's hurry!" Velma said.

We ran into the arena and climbed into the ring. Scooby-Doo sat on Mondo's chest, holding him down. The ghost had collapsed in a fit of giggles.

I turned to Malcolm Mitchell. "If we find out who's disguised as this ghost, we'll find out who kidnapped Babyface. Do you want to do the honors?"

"You bet!" Malcolm Mitchell said. He reached down and pulled the mask off Mondo's ghost.

"**T**his is delicious," Shaggy says, patting his stomach. "I could go for another helping of dessert. What about you, Scoob?"

"*Rore ressert?*" Scooby asked.

"Of course!" Shaggy said.

You look up from reading the gang's Clue Keeper.

"That was a pretty exciting case, wasn't it?" Fred asks. "You've met the suspects. You've found the clues. Do you want to try to solve the mystery?"

You nod your head.

57

"You can do it," Daphne says. "Before you start, make sure you look at your list of suspects and clues and answer these questions."

"First, who had a reason to kidnap Babyface Foster?" Velma asks.

"Second, which of the suspects do the clues point to?" Fred asks.

The waiter brings a huge dessert tray to the table. It's loaded with chocolate cake, blueberry pie, butterscotch pudding — every dessert you can name.

Shaggy licks his lips. "We'll have —"

"Two of everything, sir. I know," says the waiter. He leaves the tray on the table. "I'll get another tray."

The waiter sighs and walks away.

"It will take Shaggy and Scooby a while to finish dessert," Fred says. "Why don't you try to figure out the mystery while they're eating?"

"When you're done, we'll tell you who did it," Velma adds. "Does that sound good to you?"

You nod, then turn back to the Clue Keeper. It's just a matter of putting all the pieces into place.

Okay, it's time to solve the mystery. When you think you know who did it, turn the page.

"The man under the mask and the fake mustache was Babyface Foster," Fred says.

Babyface Foster? You were sure it was Tim Bender. And why would Babyface Foster kidnap himself, anyway?

"Tim Bender and Babyface Foster were working together," Fred explains.

"Our first clue, the makeup, told us that we were dealing with a person disguised as a ghost — not a real ghost," Velma says. "It also told us that Maxine Mitchell wasn't involved. She's allergic to makeup, remember?"

"That left Simon Blackheart and Tim

Bender," Daphne says. "When the leopard-skin costume was stolen, we figured someone stole it to use as part of the ghost costume. We thought Simon was guilty, then. After all, he had a key to the wardrobe room, just like all the other wrestlers did."

Fred leans over the table. "Tim Bender still bugged me, though. What was he doing there? Then we found out that Babyface Foster loved liver and onions and the pieces all came together."

"Malcolm Mitchell and Simon Blackheart told us that Babyface Foster was unhappy at the MWA," Velma adds. "Babyface wanted to work for Tim Bender. But he couldn't get out of his contract with the MWA. So he and Bender staged the kidnapping. That way Babyface could say the MWA put him in danger, and get out of his contract."

"Ruining the MWA's big event was just a bonus, as far as Bender was concerned," Fred adds.

"Babyface stole the makeup and the tights. He wrecked his room. Then he walked out," says Daphne.

61

"That's why we saw Mondo's ghost leave the room, but we never saw him enter," Velma explains.

"Then he hid out in Tim Bender's room," Fred says. "That's why Bender kept ordering those liver and onions."

You can't help wondering what happened at the big event. Was it ruined?

Shaggy swallows a cupcake. "Like, the crowd thought Scoob and I *were* the main event. They loved us."

Scooby-Doo nods. *"Rooby-rooby-roo!"*